Zeke Meeks
RUN! FROM BUFFY
EVIL NAILS
FAKE!
SODA
EPIC
SISTER
SNOWBALL FIGHT!
BEST FRIEND
CRIES ALOT
LA-LA-LA
ZEKE (NOT A FREAK) MEEKS
HUNTER GOING DOWN!
BULLY
SMARTY PANTS
McNUTTY
THE EMMAS
TRAINER
EWW BUGS
ME
I RULE
LITTLE SISTER
NOT A BOY
Charlie Marple
SING-A-LONG
AARRR

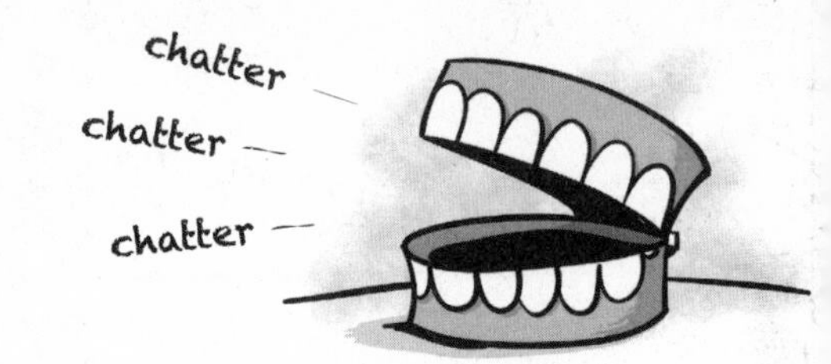

Zeke Meeks is published by
Picture Window Books
A Capstone Imprint
1710 Roe Crest Drive
North Mankato, MN 56003
www.capstonepub.com

Library of Congress Cataloging in Publication Data
Green, D. L. (Debra L.)
Zeke Meeks vs the horrendous Halloween / by D.L. Green; illustrated by Josh Alves.
p. cm. — (Zeke Meeks)
Summary: Usually Zeke loves Halloween, but this year things just seem to be going wrong—he is having trouble finding a good costume, the costume parade at school is a disaster, and he has to take his little sister trick-or-treating.
ISBN 978-1-4048-7638-5 (library binding)
1. Halloween—Juvenile fiction. 2. Middle-born children—Juvenile fiction. 3. Brothers and sisters—Juvenile fiction. 4. Elementary schools—Juvenile fiction. [1. Halloween—Fiction. 2. Middle-born children—Fiction. 3. Brothers and sisters—Fiction. 4. Elementary schools—Fiction. 5. Schools—Fiction. 6. Humorous stories.] I. Alves, Josh, ill. II. Title. III. Title: Zeke Meeks versus the horrendous Halloween. IV. Series: Green, D. L. (Debra L.) Zeke Meeks.
PZ7.G81926Zem 2013
813.6—dc23 2012028192

Vector Credits: Shutterstock
Book design by K. Fraser and K. Carlson

Printed in the United States of America in Stevens Point, Wisconsin.
092012 006937WZS13

What's got 8 legs
and a hairy body?
This guy.

Zeke Meeks
vs THE HORRENDOUS HALLOWEEN
BY D. L. GREEN
ILLUSTRATED BY JOSH ALVES

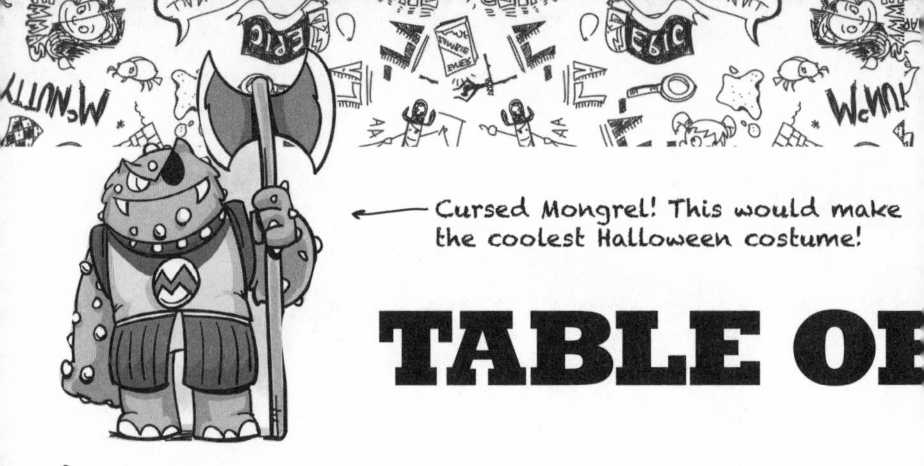

Cursed Mongrel! This would make the coolest Halloween costume!

TABLE OF

BOYS RULE EVERYTHING BUT THE PLAYGROUND

CHAPTER 1:
Singing Sisters and SCARY Spiders Are Not Super Duper 6

CHAPTER 2:
UNcool at School 18

CHAPTER 3:
The Phone Call That Changed My Life 28

CHAPTER 4:
It Was All Hector's Fault, Kind Of 38

CHAPTER 5:
Curse of the Cursed Mongrels 48

I am REALLY not a fan of bugs. At all.

Things will NEVER be the same.

So cursed, they're cursed twice

ME, TRYING TO BRAINSTORM COSTUME IDEAS . . .

UPSIDE-DOWN IS THE BOMB.

IDEAS LITERALLY FALL OUT OF YOUR HEAD.

CONTENTS

CHAPTER 6:

Argh! 62

CHAPTER 7:

How Things Went HORRIBLY Wrong 74

Like really, really WRONG.

CHAPTER 8:

Trick or Treat, SMELL My Feet, Give Me Something GOOD to Eat 84

CHAPTER 9:

Dentists, Live Dead Bodies, and Something Even Worse 94

Wait. LIVE *DEAD* bodies? What does that even mean?

CHAPTER 10:

The Next Best Thing To A Big Bag of Candy 108

Candy, candy, candy, candy, candy, candy!

Singing Sisters and SCARY Spiders Are NOT SUPER DUPER

My greatest hero is the genius who invented Halloween. It's the perfect holiday. Halloween is the only night that kids can wear cool costumes, knock on strangers' doors, and get free candy.

So I was excited when I went to the Halloween Super Duper Store with my family. Well, not *everyone* in my family was there. My dad was away, fighting bad guys on a top-secret mission. He's a soldier. Waggles, our dog, wasn't at the Halloween Super Duper Store either. If Waggles had been there, he probably would have drooled on everything, especially the hamburger costumes.

"Let's get our stuff fast. This place is horrible," Mom said.

The store was very noisy and crowded. A baby was crying, people were pushing and elbowing us, and a little girl kept shouting "I want candy now!" But I liked the Halloween Super Duper Store. It had great costumes and decorations.

My little sister, Mia, ran over to a Princess Sing-Along costume. She said, "I want to be Princess Sing-Along this year."

That wasn't exactly shocking news. Mia had dressed as Princess Sing-Along for the last two Halloweens. I wished she'd get tired of Princess Sing-Along. I'd been tired of her for years, ever since Mia first started watching the *Princess Sing-Along* TV show and screeching annoying Princess Sing-Along songs.

Mia started singing a Princess Sing-Along song in the middle of the store.

I put my finger over my lips and said, "Shh."

But Mia ignored me. She screeched, "Everyone is very special, la la la. Even people who look dreadful, la la la. Don't feel that you have to change, la la la. It's okay to act real strange, la la la."

Mom said, "Shh."

Mia finally stopped singing.

Alexa, my older sister, pointed to a bikini. She said, "I want to wear this Bathing Beauty costume."

"You're not walking around the neighborhood in a bikini," Mom said.

Alexa pointed to another costume. "How about this fairy costume?"

"A fairy in a halter top and a miniskirt? No," Mom said.

Alexa held up a cheerleader costume.

"That is the shortest cheerleading skirt I've ever seen. I'm not buying that for you. How about this one instead?" Mom pointed to a beach ball costume.

"No," Alexa said.

I picked up the beach ball costume. It was bright and round and funny. "This is perfect," I said.

"No. It's bright and round and funny," Alexa said.

"It's perfect for *me*," I said. I'd found a great costume. I bet I'd be the only kid at my school dressed as a beach ball.

"Are you sure that's the costume you want? You can't change your mind. I refuse to come back to this store until next Halloween," Mom said.

I nodded. "I'm sure this is the costume I want."

After more arguing, Mom and Alexa finally agreed on a witch costume. Mom said she'd never seen such a tight witch's dress, but at least it covered Alexa's stomach. Mom also said she needed some aspirin and a long nap.

We left the costume aisle to look for Halloween decorations for our house.

I held up a large bloody skull and said, "Let's get this."

"That's too scary. I don't want to frighten little kids," Mom said.

"I want this." Mia pointed to a scarecrow wearing a flowery hat and a pink dress.

I shook my head. "That's more of a girly decoration than a Halloween decoration."

"How about this? We can hang it on our front door," Alexa said. She picked up the very worst thing in the entire store: a big green spider.

"That will scare little kids," I said.

"I'm a little kid, and that spider doesn't scare me at all," Mia said.

Mom looked at the price tag. She said, "This is a good choice. It doesn't cost very much and it's only a little scary."

A *little* scary?

It was *extremely* scary — to me, anyway. Insects terrify me. Even plastic insects scare me. Spiders aren't really insects. They have eight legs and eight eyes, while insects have only six legs and two eyes.

But spiders' two extra legs and six extra eyes make them even scarier than insects.

The last thing I wanted on my front door was a big green spider.

But I was too embarrassed to tell anyone that. Instead, I said, "I don't like that spider."

"Why not?" Mom asked.

"Um, I don't like its size," I said. It was much too big.

Mom nodded. "You're right. It's not a good size. It's too small."

Too *small*?

Alexa picked up an even bigger green spider. It was the size of my entire body. "Here's one that's a good size. And it's on sale. It doesn't cost much more than the smaller one. See?" She thrust the gigantic spider at my face.

I ran away.

"Where are you going?" Mom called after me.

"Are you scared of a plastic spider?" Alexa asked.

"No. Of course not," I lied. "I'm just going to the bathroom." I really did have to go now. The spider had scared me so much I nearly peed my pants.

Once we brought the gigantic green spider home and hung it on our front door, I'd probably have to use the bathroom every five minutes.

UNcool at School

In class the next day, I was so excited about Halloween that it was hard to concentrate. Actually, it's always hard to concentrate in class. But it's especially hard before Halloween.

My teacher, Mr. McNutty, wrote the numbers *3*, *30*, and *300* on the whiteboard. "Let's do some math. Who knows what the common multiplier is here?" he asked.

Laurie Schneider raised her hand and said, "I'm going to be a vampire for Halloween."

"Laurie, a vampire isn't a multiplier. Vampires have nothing to do with math," Mr. McNutty said.

"Count Dracula is a vampire. *Count* Dracula. Counting is how I do math," Laurie said.

"Speaking of counting, there is only one day left before Halloween," I said.

"Laurie and Zeke, focus on math," Mr. McNutty said.

Mr. McNutty pointed to the whiteboard. "Let's get back to our figures."

"Okay. I *figure* I'll get a lot of candy," I said.

"Mr. Meeks," my teacher said.

I stopped goofing off. When Mr. McNutty called me "Mr. Meeks," I knew he was really upset with me.

He said, "I'm very close to sending you to the princi—"

The recess bell rang before Mr. McNutty could say "principal" or "principal's office" or "principality." I doubted he was going to say "principality." I didn't even know what that word meant.

But he was probably very close to sending me to the principal's office. So I was very happy the bell rang.

At recess, my best friend, Hector Cruz, and I played basketball against Owen Leach and Rudy Morse. It was a great game. The score was tied.

Then Grace Chang came over. Behind her were Emma G., Emma J., and Laurie Schneider. "It's our turn to play," Grace said.

"Yeah. It's our turn to play," Emma G. said.

"Yeah. It's our turn to play," Emma J. said.

"Our game is almost over. Wait a minute or two," I said.

Suddenly, I felt fingernails on my cheek. They weren't just ordinary fingernails. They were Grace Chang's fingernails. Grace was short and skinny, but extremely evil. Her brain was evil and her mouth was evil. But her brain and mouth weren't even in the top ten evil things about Grace.

Most evil of all were her long, sharp fingernails. She used them to rip people's faces off.

I hadn't witnessed an actual face rip-off. I didn't know any kids who had gotten their faces ripped off. But I'd heard that Grace ripped off people's faces. I'd mostly heard it from Grace.

I gave her the basketball.

Then Rudy, Owen, Hector, and I quickly walked away from her.

"I wish we didn't have to stop playing basketball. Owen and I would have won the game," Rudy said.

"No. Zeke and I would have won the game," Hector said.

"No. *We* would have won the game," Owen said.

"No. *We* would have won the game," I said.

We took turns saying this for a long time. I won't write down every time we said, "No. *We* would have won the game." I don't want to bore you to death. Trust me. We said, "No. *We* would have won the game," a *lot*.

Finally, I changed the subject. I said, "I got a great beach ball costume at the Halloween Super Duper Store."

"Cool," Hector said.

"Is the beach ball costume gross and ugly and scary?" Rudy asked.

I shook my head. "No. It isn't any of those things. It just looks like a beach ball."

"I only like gross and ugly and scary costumes," Rudy said.

"Is the beach ball costume bright and round and funny?" Owen asked.

"Yes. It's all three of those things," I said.

"It's uncool for you to wear a bright, round, and funny beach ball costume," Owen said.

I frowned. Owen was the most popular kid in third grade. He knew what was cool and what wasn't. He thought my costume was uncool. So that meant it definitely was.

"I bet your beach ball costume is cool. Do you want to trick-or-treat with me?" Hector asked.

Hector was my best friend and a nice guy. But he wasn't an expert at knowing what was cool like Owen was. I told him, "I can't trick-or-treat with you or anyone else in a beach ball costume. It's uncool." I couldn't even return the costume to the Halloween Super Duper Store. My mom had said she wouldn't go back there for another year.

I sighed. This was going to be a horrendous Halloween.

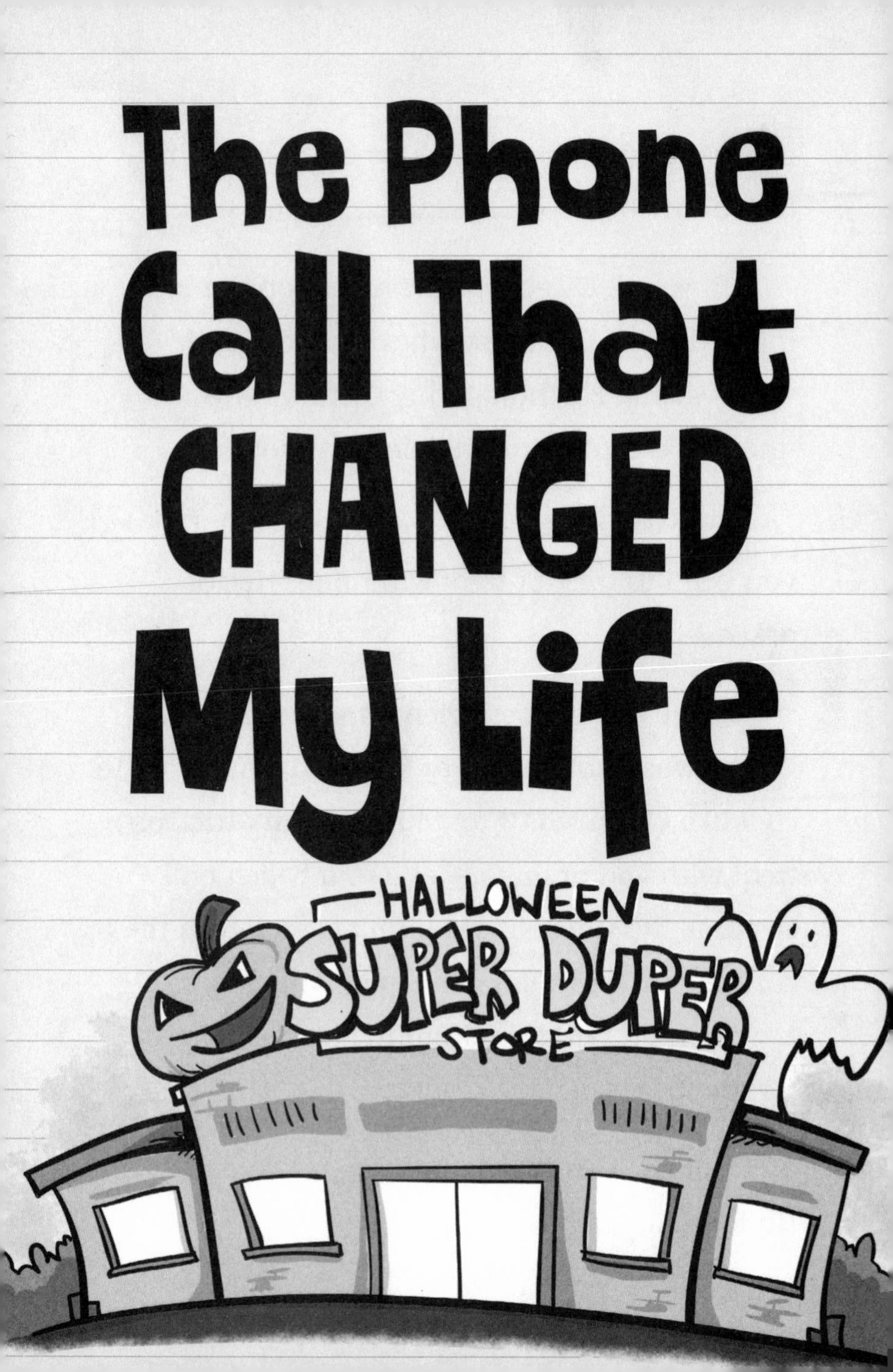
The Phone Call That CHANGED My Life
HALLOWEEN
SUPER DUPER
STORE

I was really upset for the rest of the day, even after school when I played my *Destroy, Destroy, Destroy* video game. Sure, I liked shooting at the Cursed Mongrel. But the entire time I was watching the Cursed Mongrel's warts explode all over its body, I was thinking about Halloween.

Mia got me even more upset when she sang an awful Princess Sing-Along song about Halloween: "One candy bar may taste yummy, la la la, but more than one hurts your tummy, la la la. If you eat a lot of treats, la la la, you might vomit in the streets, la la la."

"There's only one thing worse than a Princess Sing-Along song: A Princess Sing-Along song about Halloween," I said.

"Zeke, I thought you loved Halloween," Mom said.

I sighed. "I love trick-or-treating. But I can't trick-or-treat as a beach ball."

"I thought you loved the beach ball costume," Mom said.

"I did until I found out it was uncool. I wish I could exchange the beach ball costume for something better. Is there any chance that you could take me back to the Halloween Super Duper Store?"

Mom crossed her arms. "The chance of that is zero. Nil. Negative. Not going to happen. Nuh-uh. No way."

Alexa said, “The Halloween Super Duper Store is too loud and crowded. I never want to go there again.”

I frowned. “I guess I’ll stay home for Halloween. Hector will be upset. He wanted to trick-or-treat with me.”

“Maybe Hector’s parents will take you to the Halloween Super Duper Store,” Mom said.

Great idea! I hurried to the phone and called Hector.

I couldn't get through. His line was busy.

I called him again. His phone was still busy.

I clicked off the phone, but held it tight. I had to get through to Hector.

The phone rang.

"Give it to me. I'll answer it," Mom said.

"Please don't stay on the phone too long. I need to keep calling Hector," I said.

Mom picked up the telephone.

A few seconds later, she handed it to me and said, "It's Hector."

Phew. I said, "Hi, Hector. I was trying to call you, but your line was busy."

"My line was busy because *I* was trying to call *you*," Hector said.

"My dad is taking my brother and me to the Halloween Super Duper Store," he said. "Do you want to come with us? We can exchange your costume and buy costumes for us that go together."

"Hold on," I said. Then I asked my mom, "Can I go with Hector and his dad and brother to the Halloween Super Duper Store?"

Mom nodded.

"Can I come with you?" Alexa asked.

"You just told me that the store was too loud and crowded and that you never wanted to go there again," I said.

Alexa clutched her heart. "I'd go anywhere with Hector's brother. He's the cutest, coolest boy ever. His hair is amazingly silky. His arms look so strong, yet so tender. His scent is like roses mixed with leather. His —"

I cut her off. "Eww. You can't come with us. You weren't even invited."

Then I got back on the phone and told Hector, "Thanks a lot. My mom said I can go to the Halloween Super Duper Store with you."

After I got off the phone, Mom said, "Let's wait on the front porch so you'll be ready when Hector's dad gets here."

"Great idea," I said. I wanted to leave for the store as soon as I could. I grabbed the beach ball costume and the store receipt and walked outside with Mom.

She closed the front door behind us.

That's when I saw a terrifying sight: The giant green spider was hanging from our door. I felt like screaming as loud as I could and running away as fast I could.

"Are you okay? You look scared, Zeke," Mom said.

"I'm not scared," I said in a quivering voice.

Then I ran to the curb to wait for Hector, far from the terrifying spider.

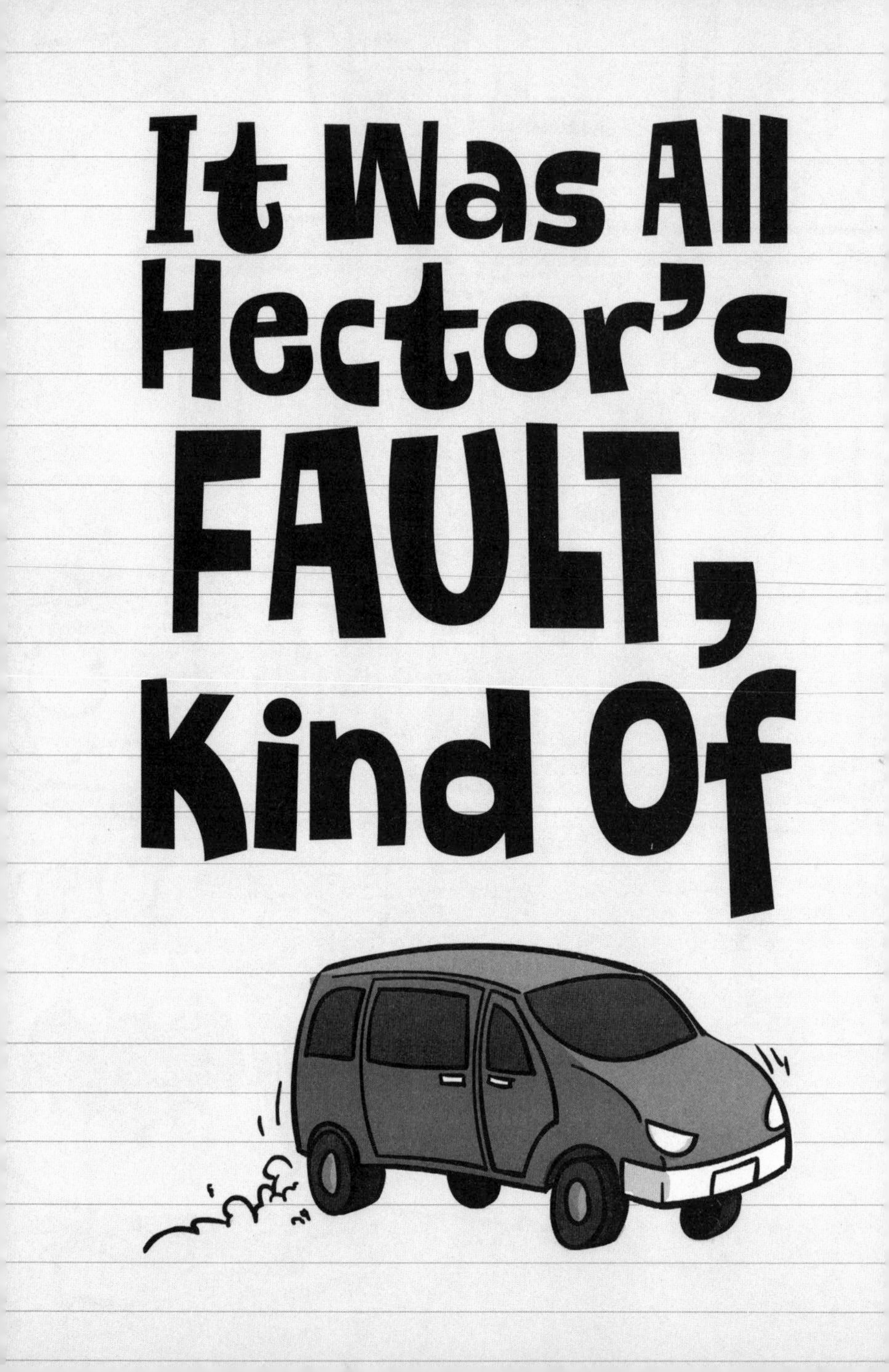
It Was All
Hector's
FAULT,
Kind Of

When Hector's dad came by, I let out a big sigh of relief. I was so happy to escape the gigantic green spider on my door.

I quickly got in the backseat of the minivan.

Hector's brother, Leon, sat in front of me. I didn't understand why my sister thought he was so great.

I took a big whiff of him. I didn't notice any leather or rose scent on him. He smelled like a regular guy.

Then I stared at him. His hair didn't look silky. It just seemed like normal hair.

I reached out and touched his arm. It felt like a regular arm to me.

Leon pushed my hand away. He turned around and asked, "What in the world are you doing?"

I blushed. "Oh. Uh. Nothing. Sorry."

I was grateful to get to the Halloween Super Duper Store. It was even more crowded and noisy today. Baby twins cried. Two kindergarten kids fought over a costume.

I told Hector, "Those babies and little kids are getting on my nerves. I'm glad we're mature now. We never scream or fight like that."

We wriggled through the mob of shoppers until we got to the costume area. I pointed to two really funny costumes. I said, "These are great for us. I'll be the plumber and you can be the toilet."

"Those are great for us only if *I* can be the plumber and *you* dress as the toilet," Hector said.

"No way," I said. Then I pointed to two more costumes. "I can be a pirate and *you* can be my parrot."

Hector shook his head. "*I'll* be the pirate and you can be *my* parrot."

"But we'll be trick-or-treating in *my* neighborhood. I don't want my neighbors to see me dressed as a parrot," I said.

"*Your* neighborhood? I thought we'd trick-or-treat in *my* neighborhood," Hector said.

"But I always trick-or-treat in my neighborhood," I said. Actually, I shouted it a little.

"*I* always trick-or-treat in *my* neighborhood," Hector shouted a little.

Hector's dad said, "Stop arguing. I want to get out of this store. Hurry and pick your costumes. You can decide later where you trick-or-treat."

Hector pointed to two other costumes. "I'll be the prince and you can be the princess."

"I'm not dressing up as a princess!" I screamed.

"Stop screaming," a little kid in a stroller told me.

"I was just kidding about you being a princess," Hector said.

"It wasn't funny. Let's just find our own costumes," I said.

"Fine." Hector crossed his arms.

"Fine." I crossed my arms.

Then I spotted the perfect costume: Cursed Mongrel.

It had slime on its head and huge warts all over its body.

It looked just like the Cursed Mongrel in my *Destroy, Destroy, Destroy* video game. I reached for the costume.

But Hector grabbed it first. He said, "This costume is perfect. It looks just like the Cursed Mongrel in my *Destroy, Destroy, Destroy* video game."

I grabbed the Cursed Mongrel costume by the arm and said, "But that's what *I* was going to wear. We can't have the same costume. It would look uncool at the school costume parade and when we trick-or-treat together."

"I picked out the Cursed Mongrel costume first," Hector said.

"That's because you were standing right next to it. I *saw* the Cursed Mongrel costume first. And I wanted it first. I should get to wear it on Halloween."

"*I* saw the Cursed Mongrel costume first," Hector said.

"*I* saw the Cursed Mongrel costume first," I said.

"*I* saw it first," Hector said loudly.

"*I* saw it first," I said loudly.

Hector's dad and big brother told us to be quiet.

But Hector and I kept arguing for a long, loud, and, quite frankly, boring time.

Finally, Hector's dad said, "You have thirty seconds left to decide on costumes. I need to get home so I can take some aspirin and a long nap. I'm never coming back here again."

Hector's brother said, "Why don't you both buy Cursed Mongrel costumes?"

"Fine!" I shouted. "We'll each trick-or-treat by ourselves in our own neighborhoods."

"Fine!" Hector shouted.

The little kid in the stroller told us again to be quiet.

"It'll be nice and quiet when I trick-or-treat by myself on Halloween," I said.

But that wasn't really true. Going trick-or-treating without my best friend might be quiet, but it wouldn't be nice.

Curse of the CURSED MONGRELS

The next day, I stared at the classroom clock. There was still an hour left before the school costume parade. I couldn't wait to show off my Cursed Mongrel costume and see what my friends were wearing.

"Zeke, pay attention. We still have an hour left of class," Mr. McNutty said.

I rested my head on my desk. How could I wait an entire hour for the parade to start?

Mr. McNutty wrote *dog, dig,* and *dug* on the whiteboard. Then he asked, "Which word comes first in the alphabet?"

I raised my hand and said, "Costume."

"Costume? I didn't write that word on the board," Mr. McNutty said.

"*Costume* stars with a *c*. *C* is the third letter of the alphabet. *D* is the fourth letter of the alphabet. So *costume* comes before *dog*, *dig*, and *dug*. I look so cool in my Halloween costume," I said.

"I look so cool in *my* costume," Hector said.

"I look the coolest of all," Owen said.

"Class. Let's get back to the lesson." Mr. McNutty pointed to the whiteboard.

Victoria Crow raised her hand. She always raised her hand. And she always knew the right answer. She was the smartest kid in third grade. She said, "*Dig* comes first in the alphabet."

"Right," the teacher said. "Now who can tell me which word comes last in the alphabet?"

"Vampire," Laurie Schneider said. "I'm going to be a vampire for Halloween."

Mr. McNutty sighed. "We know that. You interrupted the math lesson to tell us that."

"*Yowza* comes after *vampire*. People will yell 'Yowza!' when they see my totally cool costume," I said.

Victoria Crow raised her hand again. "*Yowza* isn't even a real word." She was not only the smartest kid in third grade, but often the most annoying kid, too.

"*Zombie* starts with the last letter of the alphabet. It comes after *yowza* and *vampire*. I'm going to be a zombie for Halloween," Charlie said. Charlie lived across the street from me. She was my second best friend.

"I can't wait to see your zombie costume, Charlie," I said.

Mr. McNutty rubbed his forehead. "I need some aspirin and a long nap."

"That's what my mom and Hector's dad both said at the Halloween Super Duper Store. Did you go there too?" I asked Mr. McNutty.

"I went there once, a long time ago. I'll never, ever, ever go there again," he said.

"I love that store," I said.

A lot of my classmates said they loved the store too. Some of them shouted it. I shouted it too.

Mr. McNutty sighed again. "You kids are too excited about Halloween to learn anything today. You might as well change into your costumes now."

Everyone cheered, except for Victoria. She said, "I was hoping to have an interesting discussion about alphabetical order."

I told her, "That's impossible. Alphabetical order cannot be made interesting."

Mr. McNutty sighed once again.

The boys went to the boys' bathroom to change. The girls got dressed in the girls' bathroom.

Hector and I were the first kids to get into our costumes and return to the classroom. I said, "I love my Cursed Mongrel costume. But I wish I was the only kid who had it."

"I wish *I* was the only kid with a Cursed Mongrel costume," Hector said.

Aaron Glass finished changing next. He walked into our classroom wearing a Cursed Mongrel costume.

I didn't love my costume very much anymore.

Then Danny Ford came in dressed as a Cursed Mongrel.

I didn't even *like* my costume anymore.

At least the girls dressed differently. Charlie wore a great zombie costume. Victoria Crow dressed as a scientist. Lots of girls wore princess costumes.

Then Grace Chang, Emma G., and Emma J. walked into the classroom dressed as Cursed Mongrels. I sighed even more than Mr. McNutty had.

Owen Leach entered the room next. He wore a beach ball costume.

That got me mad. I told Owen, "You said that dressing up as a beach ball was uncool. That's why I returned my costume to the store."

"Dressing up as a beach ball *is* uncool when someone else in your class does it too. I wanted to be the only kid in the class wearing a beach ball costume. And now I am." Owen smiled at me.

I frowned at him.

"I bet you guys will love my costume," Rudy Morse said from outside the classroom.

"I'll love any costume that's not another Cursed Mongrel," I replied.

Rudy Morse walked in. I did not love his costume. I did not like his costume. I despised his costume. He was dressed as a red, ugly, and very scary beetle.

I tried not to scream.

"My costume matches Cuddles, my pet beetle," he said.

"Cuddles!" I shivered in terror.

"Zeke, I'm glad you're shivering with excitement. You must love Cuddles too. He's such a great pet," Rudy said. Then he reached into the pocket of his red, ugly, and very scary beetle costume. He took out a red, ugly, and extremely scary *live* beetle. He held the beetle in front of my face and said, "Zeke, tell Cuddles you love him. Give him a big kiss."

I did not tell Cuddles I loved him. I didn't even tell Cuddles I liked him. I did not give him a big kiss or a small kiss or any kiss at all. Instead, I ran away.

I stopped near a classroom of kindergarten kids. None of them wore Cursed Mongrel costumes. But five of those little kids were dressed as beach balls.

Owen Leach was wearing a costume that was popular with kindergarteners. I smiled. Ha.

127
P

Argh!

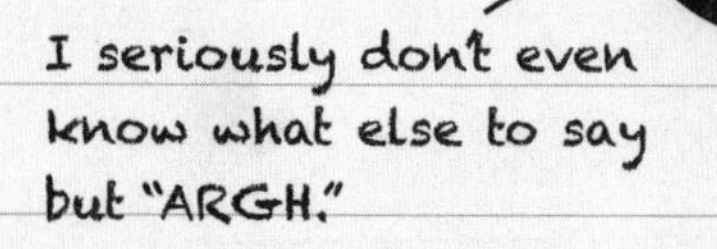
I seriously don't even know what else to say but "ARGH."

I stared at Charlie, sitting next to me in her dad's minivan as we carpooled home from school. I said, "You look like you're half dead."

Charlie smiled. "Thank you. I tried to match my makeup with my zombie costume."

"Do you want to trick-or-treat together?" I asked.

"Sure," she said.

Phew. I wouldn't get to spend Halloween with my best friend, Hector. But I'd be with my second best friend, Charlie.

Since she lived across the street from me, we wouldn't have to worry about which neighborhood to choose for trick-or-treating.

Charlie's dad dropped me off at the curb in front of my house. I walked up my driveway.

Then I saw the giant green spider hanging from my front door. I didn't want to get near that horrible thing.

"What's wrong?" Charlie called out from the minivan.

"Nothing," I said in a shaky voice. I stood, frozen, on my porch.

Suddenly, the spider swung at me.

I ducked.

I screamed.

I almost peed my pants.

“Why did you duck and scream and cross your legs when I opened the front door?” Mom asked.

“No reason.” I ran inside and into the bathroom.

After I came out, Mom asked, “How was the costume parade?”

I frowned. “It was awful. A bunch of kids were dressed as Cursed Mongrels. Can I return my Cursed Mongrel costume to the store?”

Mom shook her head. "I am not going back to the Halloween Super Duper Store. The chance of that is zero. Nil. Negative. Not going to happen. Nuh-uh. No way."

"Okay," I said, plopping down on the couch. "Maybe I can make a costume. Do you have advice on something easy to make?"

Mia came into the room. She said, "I have advice from Princess Sing-Along."

I said, "I don't want advice from Princess —"

Mia cut me off with a Princess Sing-Along song: "Scissors should be used with care, la la la. Do not toss them in the air, la la la. Don't try to eat them for dessert, la la la. They'll cut your tongue and it will hurt, la la la."

I rolled my eyes. "I wasn't planning on tossing scissors in the air or eating them for dessert."

"Don't toss scissors on the ground or eat them for breakfast or lunch either," Mia said. "I have an idea for a costume. Cut some white paper into the shape of wings. Be careful with the scissors. Tape the wings to your back and put on a white headband. You can be a pretty angel," she said.

"Thanks, but a pretty angel costume is too girly," I said.

"Here's another idea. You could make red wings with black dots and be a ladybug."

A bug? Yikes. "No thanks," I said.

"You could make black wings instead and dress as a fly," Mia said.

Flies were even scarier than ladybugs. "Can't you think of any costumes without wings?" I asked.

"You could make a pirate costume."

I nodded. "That's a great idea."

Dressing up as a pirate was easy. I made an eye patch with a string and paper. I also made a sword by covering a stick with foil. I wore a long-sleeved white shirt from my dad's closet.

Finally, Mom drew a moustache on my face with makeup and tied a bandana around my forehead. "You look great, matey," she said.

"Aye, aye," I replied. I wished I could show my costume to Hector. He really liked pirates. But Hector was trick-or-treating in his own neighborhood tonight.

After Mia got into her Princess Sing-Along costume, I said, "Yo ho ho, lassie. Let's pillage for treasure."

"I have a better idea. Stop talking that weird pirate language and let's go get candy," Mia said. "Waggles is coming too. You'll love his costume."

Waggles walked into the room. He wore Mia's ballet tutu around his stomach.

I did not love his costume. I did not even like his costume. I said, "Waggles looks ridiculous."

Mia leaned down and whispered loudly in Waggles's ear. "Don't listen to Zeke. He's jealous because you're a beautiful ballet dancer and he's not."

"Let's just go," I said.

Mom, Mia, Waggles, and I walked across the street to get Charlie and start trick-or-treating. Alexa stayed home to read her *Totally Cute Boys* magazine and pass out candy.

I rang Charlie's doorbell. After a few seconds, she opened her front door.

"Ready to trick-or-treat with me?" I asked. Before she could answer, I said,

"I'm not wearing any makeup. My face looks pale and sickly because I have the flu. I can't trick-or-treat with you," Charlie said.

"Oh, no. I hope you get better soon," I said.

Charlie's mom gave Mia and me candy. Then she closed the door behind us.

"I guess I'll spend Halloween with just you and Mia," I told Mom.

"Yay! But don't call me Mia," Mia said. "Call me Princess Sing-Along, since I'm wearing my Princess Sing-Along costume. I'm going to sing Princess Sing-Along songs all night long."

Then she sang, "Sing with me and be proud, la la la. Make sure you're nice and loud, la la la. Singing is such a terrific choice, la la la. Even if you have a screechy voice, la la la."

Mia's voice was very screechy. I thought singing was a terrible choice for her.

I also thought tonight would be the worst Halloween of my life.

How Things Went
HORRIBLY
Wrong
We're talking
MEGA FAIL!

How could a night of getting free candy go so horribly wrong?

I'll tell you how.

We left Charlie's house and walked to the next house. Mom waited on the sidewalk while Waggles, Mia, and I went to the door.

You may be asking, *What's so horribly wrong about that?*

Nothing's horribly wrong about that.

I rang the bell and Mrs. Gassman answered.

You may be asking, *What's so horribly wrong about that?*

Nothing's horribly wrong about that. Just wait.

Mia and I stuck out our bags and said, "Trick or treat."

You may be asking, *What's so horribly wrong about that?*

There's nothing horribly wrong about that, either. Don't be impatient or you'll get on my nerves.

Let's just get back to the story.

Mrs. Gassman smiled at Mia and me.

Yes, I know there's nothing horribly wrong with that, either.

Mrs. Gassman exclaimed, “A pirate and a princess! You kids look adorable! And what a pretty dog you have!”

That was how things started to go horribly wrong. First of all, I didn’t want to look adorable. I wanted to look cool, handsome, and/or awesome.

Second of all, Waggles is a boy dog. So it was an insult to call him pretty. It's true that Waggles didn't know what the word *pretty* meant. So he probably wasn't insulted. But *I* was.

Third of all, Mia said, "Thank you for calling me adorable, Mrs. Gassman. Did you know I'm not just any old princess? I'm the best princess in the land: Princess Sing-Along. Do you want to hear a Princess Sing-Along song?"

Fourth of all, Mrs. Gassman said, "I'd love to hear a Princess Sing-Along song."

Fifth of all, Mrs. Gassman ignored me when I shook my trick-or-treat bag to hint that I was waiting for candy.

Sixth of all, Mia sang a Princess Sing-Along song: "When you're in the kitchen, la la la, make the right decision, la la la. Stay away from the carving knife, la la la, unless you want to end your life, la la la."

After she finished singing, Mia said, "That's such a terrific song. Don't you agree?"

Mrs. Gassman frowned. She said, "Uh . . . well . . . um . . . let me give you your treats."

Then, seventh and worst of all, she dropped a pencil into each of our bags.

A pencil! I'd just been called adorable and heard my dog insulted and listened to Mia's song. And what did I get for all that suffering?

A lousy pencil.

Now do you see how a night of free candy could go so horribly wrong?

At almost every house, I had to wait while people said we looked adorable and Waggles looked pretty. Then I had to listen to Mia sing an awful Princess Sing-Along song.

After we'd been to about eight houses, I told Mom, "I'm tired of hearing Mia sing and people calling Waggles pretty."

Mom told me, "You've been saying that all night. I'm tired of hearing you complain."

Mia said, "I'm just tired. Can we stop trick-or-treating now?"

"But we hardly got any candy," I said.

"I can drop off Mia at home. She can help Alexa pass out candy. Then I'll take you for more trick-or-treating," Mom told me.

"Okay." I sighed. I wasn't very happy about trick-or-treating without any friends along.

Now that I was a pirate instead of a Cursed Mongrel, I wouldn't have to worry about wearing the same costume as Hector. And I would rather be with Hector in his neighborhood than without him in my neighborhood.

In my sweetest voice, I asked, "Mom, after we drop off Mia at home, can you take me to Hector's neighborhood? I want to trick-or-treat with him."

Mom shook her head. "Hector lives too far from us. I'm tired."

“Please?” I asked as sweetly as I could. I added a hopeful smile.

Mom said, “The chance of me taking you to Hector’s neighborhood is zero. Nil. Negative. Not going to happen. Nuh-uh. No way.”

I frowned. That was about the ninety-third thing that had gone horribly wrong tonight.

Trick or Treat, SMELL My Feet, Give Me Something GOOD to Eat

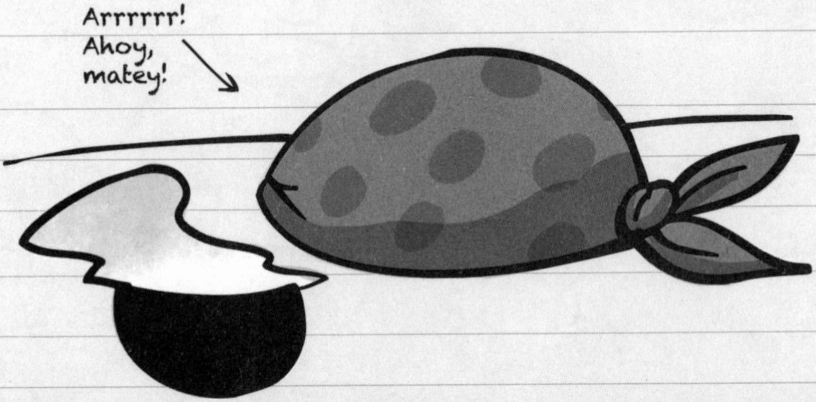

Arrrrrr!
Ahoy,
matey!

On the way home from trick-or-treating, I got an idea. That idea was called Alexa.

Alexa was sitting in the living room. She was reading *Celebrity Worship* magazine and eating the candy she was supposed to hand out.

"You know Hector's brother, right?" I asked her.

She clutched her heart. "Of course I know Hector's brother. His name is Leon."

"I wish I could know him a lot better," she continued. "He's the cutest, coolest boy ever. His eyes are like bright shining stars. His lips are like soft pillows. His bottom is like —"

"Stop," I said. "I don't want to hear about Leon's bottom. I get it. You think he's cute." I clutched my stomach. Alexa was making me feel sick.

"Leon isn't just cute. He's the cutest, coolest boy ever," Alexa said.

"Whatever. Would you like to see him tonight?" I asked.

She clutched her heart again. "On a date?"

I clutched my stomach again. "Sort of a date. You could bring me over to Leon's neighborhood. He's taking Hector trick-or-treating."

Alexa threw down her magazine, jumped off the couch, and exclaimed, "Let's go!"

"Thanks!" I hurried to the front door.

Alexa shook her head. "I meant let's go as soon as I curl my hair, polish my nails, put lip gloss on, and practice kissing moves."

I sighed. "Please hurry."

I had to wait a long time while my sister got ready to see Hector's brother. Fortunately, I had a big bowl of candy to keep me busy. I passed out candy to a few kids who came to the door. But I ate most of it myself.

Finally, Alexa was ready. I said goodbye to Mom and handed her the candy bowl. It was nearly empty. I hoped she wouldn't look inside until after we left.

Mom looked inside the bowl right away. Then she frowned and said, "Alexa Gertrude Meeks and Ezekiel Heathcliff Meeks! You ate almost all of the candy."

Alexa and I ran out of the house.

Once we stopped running, Alexa asked, "Where are we meeting Hector and Leon?"

I shrugged. "I was hoping to bump into them in their neighborhood."

"I doubt you'll find Hector and Leon that way. That's a terrible idea," Alexa said.

"If we return to our house, Mom will yell at us for eating the candy," I said.

Alexa sighed. "Let's keep going."

We were about halfway to Hector's house when I spotted him with his brother. I called out, "Hector!"

Hector waved at me, and we walked toward each other. Alexa followed me. Hector's brother followed him.

When we got closer, I said, "Nice costume, matey," at the same time Hector said, "Nice costume, matey."

Then we laughed at the same time. We were both wearing homemade pirate costumes. Hector's bandana was blue and mine was red. He had a beard and I had a moustache. Even so, we looked a lot alike.

"That's cool that we both decided to be pirates tonight," I said.

"A few days ago you told me it was uncool to dress alike," he said.

"I changed my mind. Why aren't you trick-or-treating in your neighborhood?" I asked.

"I was on my way to your neighborhood to find you."

I smiled. "*I* was on my way to *your* neighborhood to find *you*. Let's trick-or-treat together."

We walked toward the closest house.

Alexa and Leon stood frozen on the sidewalk, staring at each other.

"Oh, brother," Hector and I said at the same time. Then we said, "Jinx," at the same time. Then we both said, "Double jinx." Then we both said, "Triple jinx." Then we laughed at the same time.

After we stopped laughing, Hector asked, "Did you get much candy yet?"

I shook my head. "Hardly any. I had to wait for Mia to sing an awful Princess Sing-Along song at every house. And at one house, I got a pencil instead of candy."

"Halloween pencils should be against the law," Hector said. "I didn't get much candy, either. My mom wouldn't let me leave the house until I cleaned my room. So I started trick-or-treating late."

"I would have helped you clean your room if you'd asked," I said.

"Thanks. I'm glad we're trick-or-treating together."

I smiled again. "Me too. Now let's hurry and get as much candy as we possibly can."

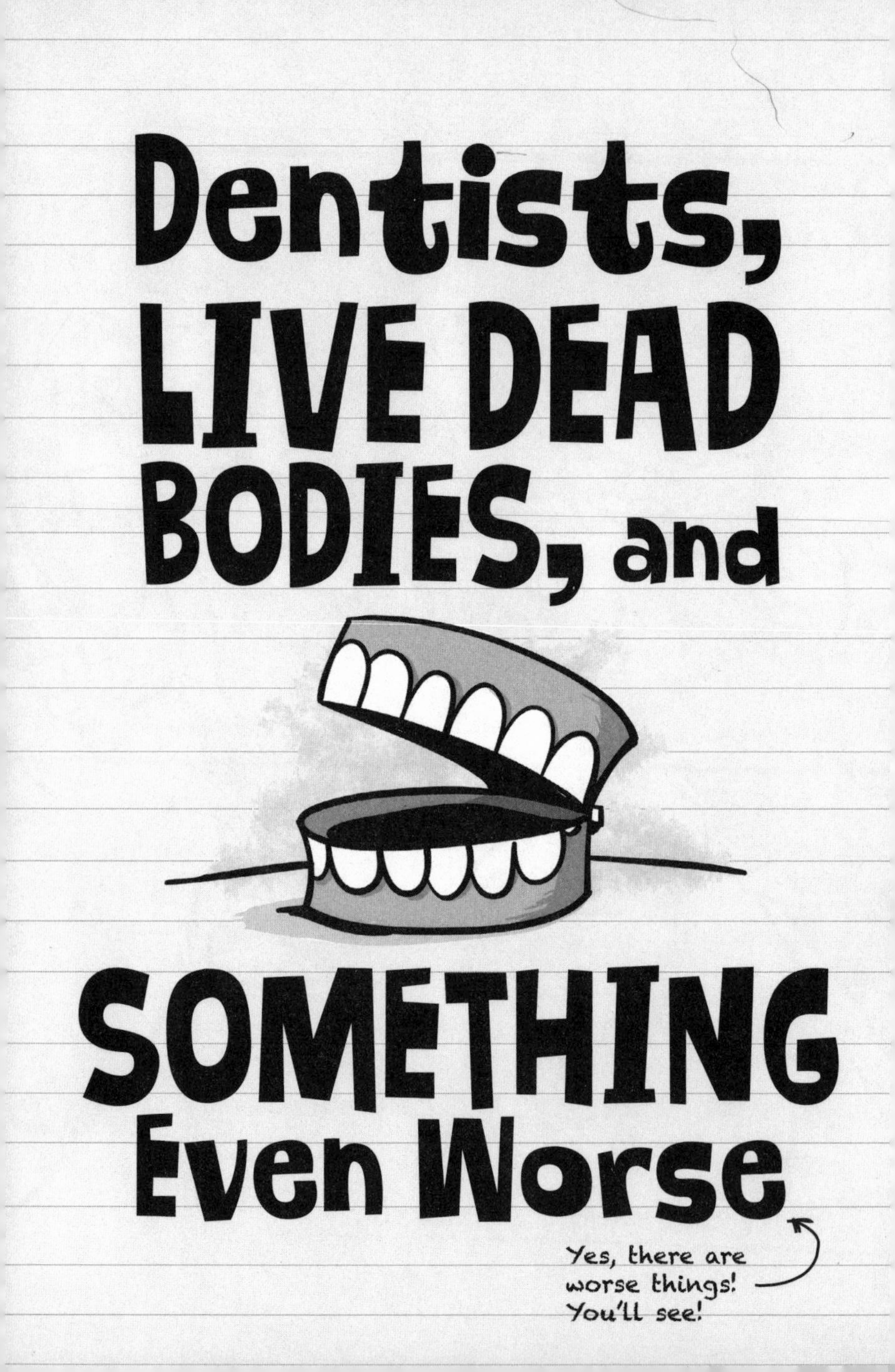
Dentists, LIVE DEAD BODIES, and
SOMETHING Even Worse
Yes, there are worse things! You'll see!

Hector and I rushed from house to house. Alexa and Leon followed us. Soon we had lots of candy corn, lollipops, jelly beans, and all kinds of chocolate bars.

I lifted my heavy trick-or-treat bag, put my face in it, and took a deep, long, wonderful whiff. Mmm. Yum. Fat and sugar. This was what Halloween was all about.

Unfortunately, we'd also gotten more pencils, an eraser, and a bag of pretzels. They were more like tricks than treats.

I raised my hand and told Hector, "I hereby vow that when I grow up, I will always give out candy on Halloween."

"Me too. And only good candy," Hector said.

I knocked on the door of a large, brightly lit house. I gasped when the door opened. Standing in front of me was Dr. Gag, my dentist.

Just thinking about Dr. Gag poking at my teeth made me shudder a little. Then I thought about his loud dental drill. I shuddered a lot.

I put my hand over my face, hoping Dr. Gag wouldn't recognize me. I mumbled, "Trick or treat."

"I recognize you. You're Zeke Meeks," Dr. Gag said.

I nodded, making sure to keep my mouth closed.

"Let me see those teeth of yours. Open your mouth," Dr. Gag said.

I did.

"Wider," he ordered.

I opened my mouth wider. I wished I had never knocked on Dr. Gag's door.

Dr. Gag peered inside. He said, "You need to come to my office as soon as possible. It looks like you have tooth and gum decay and cavities."

Then Dr. Gag pointed to Hector and said, "Open your mouth, young man."

Hector sighed. Then he opened his mouth.

Dr. Gag looked inside and said, "Young man, you have an overbite. You need braces."

Then he looked inside my trick-or-treat bag and said, "You should get rid of that awful, teeth-rotting candy. And make sure to brush after every meal and floss every day."

"I'll do that," I lied.

"Happy Halloween. Here's a special treat for you boys." He put a toothbrush in each of our bags. We thanked him and hurried away.

After we joined Leon and Alexa on the sidewalk, I said, “A toothbrush is not a treat.”

“It’s more like a bad trick,” Hector said.

“Alexa is a wonderful treat,” Leon said.

Alexa clutched her heart again. She said, “It’s a wonderful treat to see you tonight, Leon.”

Hector and I clutched our stomachs and pretended to throw up.

Then we walked toward the next house. Loud, spooky music played on outside speakers. Spider webs and skeletons hung from the trees in the front yard. A fake dead body lay on the lawn.

"This house is so cool," Hector said.

"Yeah. That fake dead body almost looks real," I replied.

Suddenly, the fake dead body sat up. She yelled, "How dare you call me a fake dead body? I'm real and alive. And now I'm very, very angry."

Hector and I ran away.

"I was just kidding, kids," the real, live and very, very angry woman called after us.

We stopped running. "Were you scared?" Hector asked.

"Me? Scared?" I said. The words came out like little squeaks. I added, "I was, uh, just getting some exercise."

"Me too. Exercise," Hector said in a little, squeaky voice.

"Hector! Zeke! Come back here! Don't you want to trick-or-treat?" Leon called to us.

Did I want to go back to the house with the very, very angry woman on the lawn? The chance of that was zero. Nil. Negative. Not going to happen. Nuh-uh. No way.

I said, "Uh, I'm kind of tired. Hector, you can go back there. I'll wait here." My voice was still little and squeaky.

"I'm not going back to the house with the real, live, and very, very angry woman. I'm ready to go home," Hector said. His voice was still little and squeaky too.

I called out, "We're done trick-or-treating."

"We're ready to go home," Hector said.

Alexa and Leon walked toward us. They were holding hands.

Hector and I pretended to throw up again.

"Don't go yet, Leon," Alexa said.

“I don’t want to go, Alexa,” Leon said. Then he put his arms around her and —

I’d better prepare you for this first.

What you’re about to read is totally gross.

It’s even grosser than the huge green spider on my door.

Don’t read this if you’re eating.

Are you near a bathroom or trash can? You should be, in case you need to throw up.

If you’re not near a bathroom or trash can, I’ll wait while you find one.

Ready?

Okay. I’ll tell you.

Alexa and Leon pressed their mouths on each other, like plungers on toilets. They kissed and kissed for a very long, disgusting time.

It was a horrible display of total grossness. I almost threw up.

Just typing this now is making me feel queasy.

"Let's get out of here," I said.

"We're done trick-or-treating," Hector said.

Alexa and Leon kept kissing.

"Mom is going to be mad if you don't take me home soon," I told Alexa.

"Yeah, same here," Hector told Leon.

But Alexa and Leon kept on kissing.

There was only one thing to do: Hector and I sat on the sidewalk, opened our bags, and started eating our candy.

RIP

The Next Best THING to a BIG BAG of Candy
NOM NOM NOM
NOM NOM NOM
NOM NOM!!
CHOCO
LATE

Alexa and Leon kissed and kissed and kissed. Yuck and yuck and yuck.

Meanwhile, Hector and I ate and ate and ate. Hector held up a chocolate bar and said, "Eww. This has coconut in it. I despise coconut."

"How could anyone not like the light, tasty goodness of coconut? Not just anyone, but my best friend. It's hard to believe," I said.

"Believe it. I'll trade my coconut candy for some of your candy," Hector said.

I held up a square of caramel. "How about this? I despise caramel."

"I can't believe my best friend doesn't like the sweet, chewy goodness of caramel," Hector said.

We soon traded all kinds of candy: Hector's Reese's Pieces for my Tootsie Rolls; his Kit Kats for my Heath bars; and his red and purple lollipops for my yellow and orange ones.

The entire time, Alexa and Leon were kissing. Yuck.

I had just traded my Snickers bars for Hector's Skittles when we saw Owen Leach. He was waddling toward us very slowly.

Finally, he stopped in front of us. He looked in our bags and said, "You guys got a lot of candy."

"Yeah, and we already ate a lot of it," I said.

"How about you? Did you get much candy?" asked Hector.

Owen frowned. "I hardly got any. This beach ball costume is really hard to walk in. It took me a long time to get to each house."

I held back a smile. Owen didn't deserve much candy. He'd told me my beach ball costume was uncool just because he wanted to wear it.

"Did you trick-or-treat with other kids?" Hector asked.

Owen shook his head. "I started trick-or-treating with my neighbors. But they got tired of waiting for me. So I went with just my mother. When we got to Dr. Gag's house, my mom set up a dental appointment for me. Dr. Gag thinks I need three cavities filled."

It was really hard not to smile now.

"Hurry up, Owen!" a woman shouted.

Owen sighed. "That's my mother. Even *she's* tired of waiting for me. See you later." He slowly waddled away.

I glanced at Alexa and Leon. They were still kissing. I quickly looked away.

Hector and I ate more candy. After awhile, I rubbed my stomach and said, "I never thought it was possible to eat too much candy. But I think I just did. I feel sick."

"Me too. And hearing Alexa and Leon swap spit makes me feel even more sick," Hector said.

"We'd better stop them before we throw up," I said.

I stood behind Alexa. Hector stood behind Leon. We each put our arms around their waists and pulled them apart.

"It's late. We have to go," I said.

"Oh, Leon. This has been, like, the best night ever," Alexa said.

"Like, barf," I said.

"How about a kiss goodbye?" Leon asked Alexa.

"Barf," Hector said.

"You've done enough kissing for one night," I said.

"You've done enough kissing for a *thousand* nights," Hector said.

Hector and I led Alexa and Leon away from each other.

"Bye, Zeke," Hector said as we walked toward our own neighborhoods.

"I hate to leave you, my darling Hector," I joked.

Hector laughed and said, "Now I'm really going to throw up."

As we made our way home, I told Alexa, "Thanks for taking me trick-or-treating."

She clutched her heart again. "Thanks for helping me meet my true love. This was the best night of my life."

“It wasn’t the best night of my life. But it was in the top twenty,” I said.

It hadn’t been a perfect Halloween. I had switched costumes at the last minute. Dr. Gag had lectured me about my teeth. I got pencils, an eraser, a toothbrush, and other terrible tricks. I was terrified by a dead body that turned out to be alive. I got sick from too much candy and from the awful sight of Alexa and Leon kissing.

But going through those things with my friend Hector made them a lot better. A good friend was almost as good as a big bag of candy.

Once we got to our block, I said, “Wait a minute, Alexa. I need to do something.”

Then I walked to Charlie’s house and rang the doorbell.

Charlie's mom answered. She said, "Hello, Zeke. Didn't I already give you candy tonight?"

"That's not why I'm here. How's Charlie?"

"She's still sick, but it doesn't seem that bad," she said.

"I'm sorry she didn't get to trick-or-treat tonight. I'm also sorry I didn't get to hang out with her. Do you have a bag I can use?" I asked.

"Sure, Zeke." Charlie's mom gave me a grocery bag.

I poured half my candy into it. "This is for Charlie. Please tell her I hope she gets well soon."

Her mom smiled. "That was nice of you."

"I know," I said as I walked away.

STUFF
MART

Alexa and I went across the street to our house. Alexa said, “That was nice of you.”

“I know,” I said.

“You’re really growing up,” she said.

I was about to say, “I know,” again. But, suddenly, I couldn’t talk. I was too scared of the giant green spider hanging on our front door.

ABOUT THE AUTHOR

D. L. Green lives in California with her husband, three children, silly dog, and a big collection of rubber chickens. She loves to read, write, and joke around.

ABOUT THE ILLUSTRATOR

Josh Alves's favorite kind of candy is Peanut Butter M&Ms and he loves making costumes with his kids. Josh gets to draw fun stuff at his studio in Maine where he lives (and trick-or-treats) with his amazing wife and three incredible children.

WHY DO PEOPLE GIVE LAME TREATS ON HALLOWEEN?

(And other really important questions)

Write answers to these questions, or discuss them with your friends and classmates.

1. Why do people give bad treats on Halloween? What is the worst treat you ever got?

2. It took me a long time to figure out a Halloween costume. Do you think it is easy or hard to find the perfect costume?

3. What are some of your all-time favorite costumes?

4. My fight with Hector almost destroyed my Halloween. Have you ever fought with your best friend? What happened?

5. Have you ever seen anything grosser than Alexa and Leon kissing? (I seriously doubt it, but have you?!)

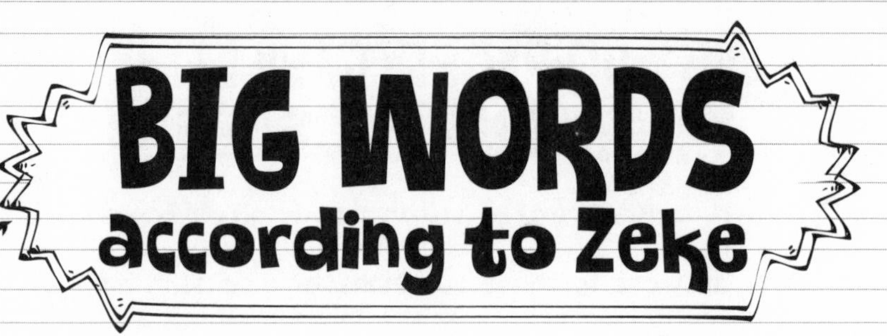

TRY USING THEM IN SENTENCES JUST LIKE I DO

ADORABLE: A word that girls use to describe things that they think are super cute. But adorable things are actually usually annoying and somewhat gross.

ANNOYING: Things that are annoying bug you so much you think you might lose it!

CONCENTRATE: To think really hard while you work on something. When I play video games, I concentrate hard. When I learn about math . . . not so much.

DEFINITELY: For sure and without a doubt. For example, Princess Sing-Along is definitely awful.

DESPISE: If you hate something more than anything you have ever, ever, ever hated before, they you actually despise it.

DISCUSSION: To talk about something with someone else. Discussions tend to be long and often boring.

DREADFUL: Super duper awful, like when someone gives you a toothbrush for a Halloween treat.

ELBOWING: Sticking out your elbows to get some room for yourself.

EXTREMELY: Super duper, very much so.

EXTREMELY cool costume . . .
until everyone wears it

GENIUS: A genius is VERY smart and knows a lot about everything. They can use their knowledge for good and invent things like Halloween. Or they can show off and bore everyone like Victoria Crow.

GIGANTIC: Big, huge, large beyond belief.

HORRENDOUS: Truly and completely awful.

IGNORED: When I get ignored, people act like they can't hear me or even see me. RUDE!

IMPATIENT: Unable to wait without being crabby about it.

INSULTED: Said or did something that made a person feel bad. Every time my sisters dress Waggles up, I am totally insulted.

LOUSY: Bad and lame. Things that are lousy include toothbrushes and pencils as treats, being sick on Halloween, and Mia's singing.

MULTIPLIER: Not so sure what this is, but it has to do with math and multiplication. Maybe check with Victoria.

QUIVERING: Shaking out of fear, like when I see, hear, or think about insects.

RIDICULOUS: very silly and just not right, like Waggles in girly clothes.

SCREECHING: Loud and high-pitched and awful! In other words, everything that has to do with Princess Sing-Along.

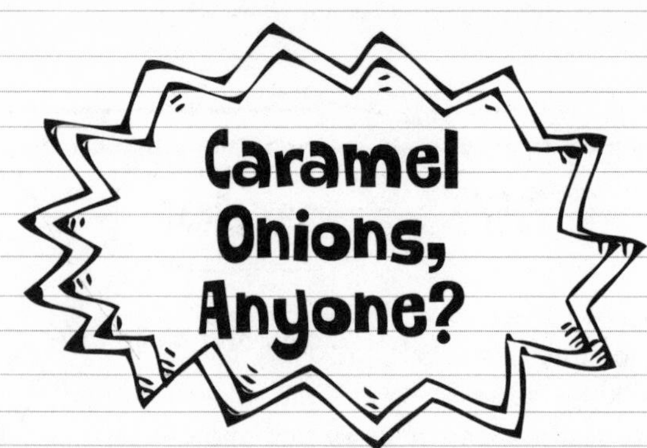

That lady who pretended to be a fake dead body on her lawn got me thinking. Halloween is a great time for pulling pranks: you could blame the pranks on ghosts and goblins and hopefully not get in trouble.

I'm going to make these caramel onions to trick Mia and Alexa. And I'm going to ask mom for help. I'd be in HUGE trouble if I tried this without permission.

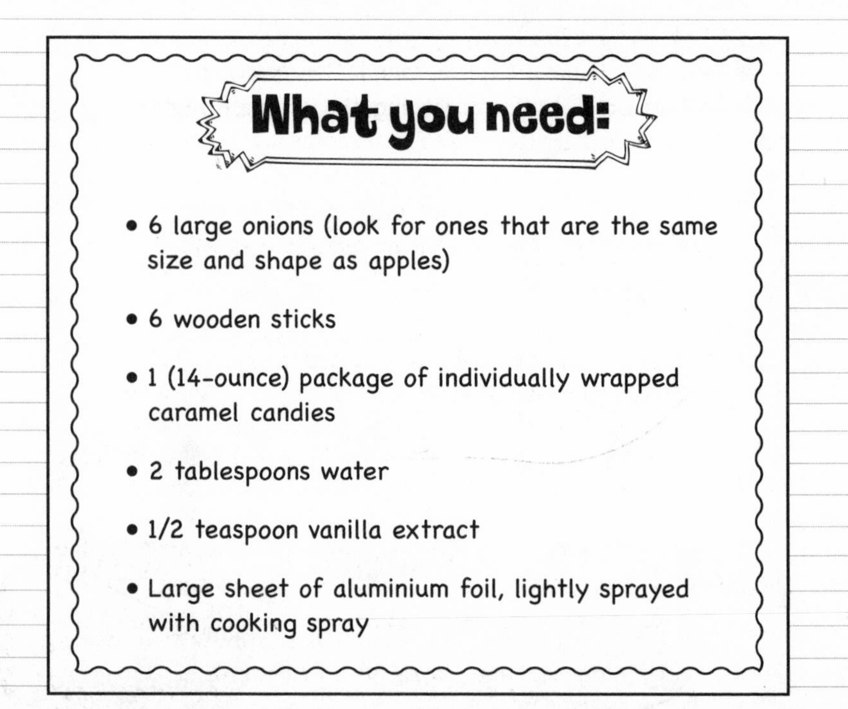

What you need:

- 6 large onions (look for ones that are the same size and shape as apples)
- 6 wooden sticks
- 1 (14-ounce) package of individually wrapped caramel candies
- 2 tablespoons water
- 1/2 teaspoon vanilla extract
- Large sheet of aluminium foil, lightly sprayed with cooking spray

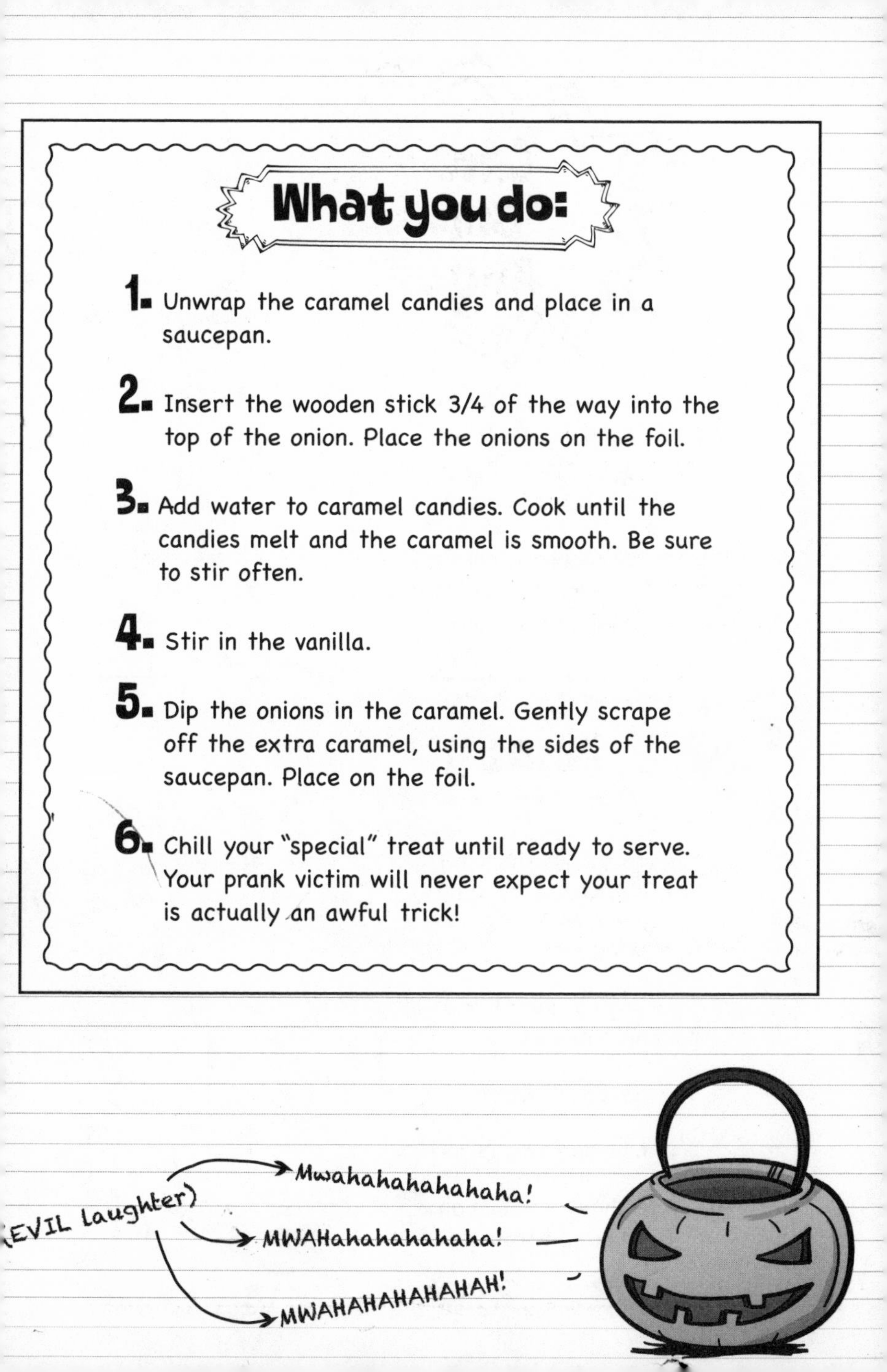

What you do:

1. Unwrap the caramel candies and place in a saucepan.

2. Insert the wooden stick 3/4 of the way into the top of the onion. Place the onions on the foil.

3. Add water to caramel candies. Cook until the candies melt and the caramel is smooth. Be sure to stir often.

4. Stir in the vanilla.

5. Dip the onions in the caramel. Gently scrape off the extra caramel, using the sides of the saucepan. Place on the foil.

6. Chill your "special" treat until ready to serve. Your prank victim will never expect your treat is actually an awful trick!

AWESOME HAIR
CHARMING SMILE
Zeke Meeks
COOLEST THIRD GRADER YOU'LL EVER MEET!